A Perfect
Time for Pandas

MAGIC TREE HOUSE® #48
A MERLIN MISSION

A Perfect Time for Pandas

by Mary Pope Osborne

illustrated by Sal Murdocca

SCHOLASTIC INC.

ISBN 978-0-545-78457-3

12 11 10 9 8 7 6 5 4 3 2 1   14 15 16 17 18 19/0

Printed in the U.S.A.   40

First Scholastic printing, September 2014

To Andy Boyce, who loves pandas

CONTENTS

Prologue

One summer day in Frog Creek, Pennsylvania, a mysterious tree house appeared in the woods. It was filled with books. A boy named Jack and his sister, Annie, found the tree house and soon discovered that it was magic. They could go to any time and place in history just by pointing to a picture in one of the books. While they were gone, no time at all passed back in Frog Creek.

Jack and Annie eventually found out that the tree house belonged to Morgan le Fay, a magical librarian from the legendary realm of Camelot. They have since traveled on many adventures in the magic tree house and completed many missions for both Morgan le Fay and her friend Merlin the magician. Teddy and Kathleen, two young enchanters from Camelot, have sometimes helped Jack and Annie in both big and small ways.

Now Teddy and Kathleen are in urgent need of Jack and Annie's help. While Merlin and Morgan were away from Camelot, Teddy accidentally put a spell on Penny, Merlin's beloved penguin, turning her into a statue. Teddy is sure he will be banished from Camelot unless Jack and Annie can help save Penny.

Teddy and Kathleen have found an ancient spell that will undo Teddy's accidental magic. To make the spell work, Jack and Annie must find four special objects, each from a different time and place. They have found three of these objects—and now they are waiting to find out where they must go next, and what they must find. . . .

CHAPTER ONE

The Fourth Thing

Jack heard knocking on his door. *Teddy and Kathleen were knocking! They were calling to him! He had to help them save Penny!* Jack tried to cross his room . . . but his legs wouldn't move. He couldn't get to the door!

The knocking grew louder. "Jack?" his dad called.

Jack opened his eyes. Where was he?

"Jack, get up! School!" came his dad's voice.

What a dream, thought Jack. He quickly sat up in bed. He'd overslept!

"Jack? Are you awake?" said his dad, peeking into his room.

"Yep, thanks, Dad!" said Jack.

"Better hurry," said Jack's dad. He closed the door.

Jack hopped out of bed. *Where's Annie?* he wondered. They had planned to go to the tree house before school! Today was the day to find the fourth thing to save Penny.

Jack pulled on his jeans and a T-shirt and rushed out of his room. Annie charged out of *her* room at the same moment. "We overslept!" she said.

"No kidding," said Jack. "Hurry! We have to get to the tree house before school starts."

"I know!" said Annie.

Annie and Jack charged down the steps. They rushed into the kitchen.

"Good morning, sleepyheads," their mom said. "You have just enough time for breakfast. I made you egg sandwiches."

"Thanks, Mom," said Jack. "But would you mind if we take them with us? We have to head to school early. We have a special project."

"You guys really seem to love school," their dad said.

"Yep, school's great," said Jack.

Their mom wrapped up their sandwiches and put them in a paper bag. She handed the bag to Annie. "You two have a good day," she said.

"Thanks, Mom!" said Annie.

Jack and Annie hurried to the front door and stepped outside into the moist spring air.

"We have exactly twenty-five minutes before we have to head to school," Jack said.

"No problem," said Annie. "Hold on." She put their sandwiches in Jack's backpack. "Okay. Let's go!" They raced across their yard and charged up the sidewalk. They ran across the street and headed into the Frog Creek woods. They ran between trees full of new green leaves until they came to the tallest oak.

The magic tree house was high up in the branches. Annie grabbed the rope ladder and started up. Jack followed. Inside the tree house they both sat on the floor, catching their breath.

"Whew . . . it's all still here," gasped Annie.

Dusty rays of morning light shone through the tree house window onto the three things they'd already found to help Teddy and Kathleen: a rose carved out of an emerald from India, a dried white and yellow flower from the Swiss Alps, and a goose-feather quill pen from President Abraham Lincoln.

"I hope Teddy and Kathleen were able to translate the last part of the rhyme," said Jack. "Do we have a new note?"

They both looked around the tree house. "Aha!" said Annie. She pointed to a book and a small scroll lying in the corner.

Jack picked up the book, and Annie grabbed the scroll. "Interesting," said Jack. He showed the cover of the book to Annie.

"Cool, China!" said Annie.

"We've been there before," said Jack. "Remember the emperor who burned the books and tried to have us killed?"

"That was more than two thousand years ago," said Annie. "Maybe we're going to a different time now."

Annie unrolled their scroll and read aloud:

Dear Jack and Annie,
    We haven't yet finished translating the last lines of the secret rhyme to reverse the statue spell Teddy cast on Penny. But we do know the fourth object we need to break the

spell. And we know that it can be found in Southwest China. It is:

A healthy food, grainy and good,
baked with love, tough as wood,
round in shape, the color of sand,
given to those who have lost their land.

Once you have found the last object,
please hurry to Camelot. Morgan and Merlin
will return by break of day tomorrow!
                    —Teddy and Kathleen

"Healthy food in China?" said Annie. "That shouldn't be hard to find."

"But don't you think it sounds kind of weird?" said Jack. "How can anyone eat something that's tough as wood?"

"Good question," said Annie. "But we'll have fun looking for it. I love the food we get with Mom and Dad at Chinatown Palace, don't you?"

"Yeah . . . but . . . ," said Jack.

"Okay!" said Annie. "Now, did Teddy and Kathleen send a potion or anything else magical to help us?"

Jack looked around the tree house again.

"There!" he said. A small glass bottle glinted in a shadowy corner. Jack picked it up, and he and Annie stepped to the window and read the writing on the bottle's label.

Use only once. Take one sip and grow to five times your size. The magic lasts for one hour.

"Five times our size?" said Jack. "That would make us about as tall as a house."

"Talk about weird," said Annie.

"Yeah, but it actually sounds like fun," said Jack.

"More fun than when we became teeny-tiny in India," asked Annie, "after we saw the cobras?"

"*Lots* more," said Jack, "especially if we have to get away from cobras again." He put the rhyme and the tiny bottle into his backpack, then took a deep breath. "Okay! All set?"

"Ready," said Annie.

Jack pointed to the cover of the guide book. "I wish we could go there!" he said.

The wind started to blow.

The tree house started to spin.

It spun faster and faster.

Then everything was still.

Absolutely still.

CHAPTER TWO

Silly Food

It was daylight outside. A rooster crowed in the distance. The air was damp and cool.

"Good, it's really early," said Jack. "So we have a whole day and night until break of day *tomorrow* to do our mission."

"Perfect," said Annie. "And look—we get to wear our own clothes for once."

"Oh, man," said Jack. He was still in his jeans and T-shirt, and his backpack was still a backpack. "Is that a mistake?"

Jack and Annie looked out the window together.

Mountains rose majestically above the town they had landed in. The tree house was in the tallest tree in a grove at the edge of a quiet street. Along the street were shops and other buildings—and a few cars.

"Cars!" Jack said with relief.

"No mistake," said Annie. "Our clothes didn't change because we came to China in modern times."

Jack reached into his pocket and pulled out some paper money. "Cool, my clothes didn't change, but my money changed from dollars to Chinese money."

"Perfect," said Annie. She looked out the window again and read some signs from the buildings: "Wolong Town Bank, Wolong Town School, Wolong Town Bicycle Shop. I think we landed in Wolong Town."

"Wow," said Jack. "How did you figure that out?"

Annie laughed. "So let's go look for some Wolong Town food."

"Okay, but the food we have to find doesn't sound like normal food," said Jack. " 'Grainy and good' but 'tough as wood'?"

Annie smiled. "You always find *something* to worry about," she said. "Come on."

Annie headed down the tree house ladder. Jack packed away their book in his backpack and followed her. Together, they stepped out from the grove of trees and headed down a busy sidewalk.

Vendors were setting up stalls to sell crafts and pottery. Some girls and boys were passing by, carrying book bags. They were dressed in jeans, T-shirts, and sweatshirts.

"See, kids just like us, on their way to school,"
said Annie.

"Except we took a detour to have breakfast halfway around the world," said Jack.

"Speaking of breakfast—how about going *there*?" Annie pointed to a restaurant with tables outside.

"Garden Paradise?" Jack said, reading the sign. "Sounds like a good place to start."

Jack and Annie crossed the street to the restaurant. Tables were set up near potted bamboo plants. A waiter poured tea for someone reading a newspaper. Jack glanced at the front page of the paper and saw the date.

"It's May 12, 2008," he said.

"Cool," said Annie.

The waiter nodded at Jack and Annie. Then he led them to a table that had two small bowls on it. "Green tea?" he asked. "Or yak butter tea?"

Jack and Annie answered together: "Green!"

The waiter left and came back with a teapot. He poured pale green tea into two small bowls. Then he gave Jack and Annie menus and went to check on other customers.

"Yak butter tea?" Jack said. "I don't think so."

Annie giggled as she looked at her menu. "Hmm! How about some green bean jelly? I don't think so."

Jack scanned his menu. "Aha! What about chicken feet?"

"Eww!" said Annie.

"Okay. How about *this*?" Jack said gleefully. *"Fried stinky tofu?"*

"EWW!" said Jack and Annie together. They laughed loudly, and Annie nearly fell out of her chair.

Jack saw the waiter frowning at them from across the garden. "Shhh," Jack said. "We're being rude."

"Sorry, sorry," Annie whispered in the direction of the waiter. "We have funny-sounding food at home, too," she said to Jack. "Like hot *dogs*."

"Oh, yeah. How about *sour* cream?" said Jack. "Or *squash*?"

"Ahh! Squash!" Annie laughed.

"Okay, okay. Let's get serious now," said Jack. "We have a mission." He took the little scroll from his pack, unrolled it, and read:

> *A healthy food, grainy and good,*
> *baked with love, tough as wood,*
> *round in shape, the color of sand,*
> *given to those who have lost their land.*

"It's a riddle," said Annie.

"It is," said Jack. "Maybe we should just ask the waiter for help." He waved politely in the waiter's direction.

When the waiter came to the table, he gave them a tight smile. "Are you ready to order now?" he asked.

"Actually, we have some questions," said Jack.

The waiter nodded.

"Do you serve food that's the color of sand?" Annie asked.

The waiter stared at her.

Jack felt awkward. "Or, um, food that's . . . like, um, as tough as wood?" he said.

"Food like sand and wood?" the waiter said.

"Not exactly—" Jack said.

"Are you trying to be funny?" the waiter inter-
rupted. He gave Jack a fierce look.

Sinking down in his chair, Jack shook his head.

"Well, the answer is *no*," said the waiter. "We
do not have such silly food!"

"Oh. Okay," said Jack.

"Is there something else you would like?" the
waiter asked.

"No thanks," said Jack. He could feel his face
turning red.

The waiter slapped their check on the table
and walked away.

"Whoa. We should leave," said Jack, standing
up. He looked at the check, then took a twenty-
yuan note out of his pocket and left it on the table. "Come on." He walked quickly around the
tables to the exit. Annie hurried after him.

Back on the sidewalk, Jack sighed. "So, where
do we go to look for this weird food now?"

"Maybe the guide book can help us," Annie
said.

"Maybe," said Jack. He pulled out their book

and looked up *Wolong Town* in the index. He turned to a page and read aloud:

> Wolong (say WOO-long) means "sleeping dragon." Wolong Town is inside the Wolong National Nature Reserve, which is circled by a mountain range called the Sleeping Dragon. According to legend, a dragon fell in love with the beauty of the mountains and trees. He curled around them to take a nap and never woke up.

"That's cool," said Annie.

"Yeah, but it doesn't help us," said Jack. He read more:

> Wolong Reserve is home to rare Asian animals such as giant pandas, golden snub-nosed monkeys, white-lipped deer, and—

"Wait! Back up!" said Annie. "Did you say giant pandas?"

"Yes . . . ," said Jack.

"Oh my gosh!" said Annie. She covered her heart with her hands. "My life's dream has *finally* come true!"

"What life's dream?" said Jack, looking at her. "Pandas?"

"Yes! I've *always* wanted to see real pandas up close! Haven't you?" said Annie. She took the guide book and flipped through the pages until she found photos of pandas. She read aloud:

In 1980, the Conservation and Research Center for the Giant Panda was set up in the Wolong Reserve to be a safe haven for the animals.

"A panda center! We *have* to go there!" said Annie. "Now!"

"Wait, wait," said Jack. "We have a mission! Why are you acting so crazy about pandas?"

"I can't help it," said Annie. "All my life I've wanted to meet real pandas. Remember my two stuffed animals? Roly and Poly? I loved them so much! You know that!"

"Okay, okay. But we have to stick to our mission," Jack said.

"We have lots of time to find that special food," said Annie. "Wolong has other restaurants. It can't be that hard to find a weird food. Hey! I have a good idea!" She gave the guide book back to Jack, then started off. "Come with me!"

"Wait, stop. Where are we going?" Jack said.

"We passed a bicycle shop earlier," Annie called over her shoulder. "I'll bet they rent bikes!"

"What? Are you crazy?" Jack put their book away and walked after her. "Where is this panda center?" he called. "We might not have enough time to get there and back *and* complete our mission. Plus renting bikes costs money. We don't know how much."

"Let's find out!" said Annie. She started running up the street to the Wolong Town Bicycle Shop.

CHAPTER THREE

The Sleeping Dragon

Oh, brother, thought Jack, hurrying after Annie. By the time he entered the bike shop, she was already talking with the man who worked there. "Good news!" Annie said, rushing over to Jack. "He says we *can* get to the panda center on mountain bikes! And it's only thirty yuan a day per bike!"

"Did he say how long it takes to get there?" asked Jack.

"Not too long," said Annie. She clapped her hands. Her eyes were shining. "Jack! I can't believe this!"

Annie was so excited about the panda center that Jack just couldn't say no. He reached into his pocket and took out three twenty-yuan notes and gave them to the shopkeeper.

The man handed Jack and Annie their helmets. "It's a beautiful ride up the mountain, but be *very* careful," he said as Annie put her helmet on.

"Thanks! See you later!" said Annie. She grabbed a blue mountain bike and steered it out of the store.

"Be very careful!" the man called after her again.

Very careful of what? wondered Jack. But tucking his helmet under his arm, he grabbed a red bike and followed Annie.

"So the bike guy told me to go up this street and turn left onto the highway," Annie said. "Then we just stay on it until we come to the panda center."

"Cool. How far away is it?" asked Jack as he put on his helmet. He snapped the strap under his chin.

"Not far, just five or six miles," said Annie.

"*What?*" said Jack.

"Don't worry, we can do it. Easy." Annie pushed off and pedaled away. "To panda paradise!" she shouted, zooming up the street.

"Five or six miles," muttered Jack. "Up a mountain. Great." He got on his bike and followed Annie. She reached the end of the street and turned left onto the highway. Jack hurried to catch up. As he pedaled up the highway, he glanced at the scenery.

On one side of the road was a steep mountain slope. It was covered with fir trees and bushes with purple and pink flowers. On the other side of the road was a steep drop down into a river valley. The river sparkled with sunlight as it rushed through green farmland. More cloud-covered mountains loomed in the distance.

A blue bus suddenly roared past. Jack almost lost his balance. "Good grief!" he said. "That was close!"

Then a car that looked like a taxi flew by. "This is definitely not safe!" Jack said aloud. How could he have let Annie talk him into riding bikes on a highway? They should have taken a bus or a taxi, or better yet, not gone at all!

"Annie!" Jack shouted. She was so far ahead that he could barely see her. "Annie!" Jack yelled again as loudly as he could. "Slow down! Annie! Slow down!"

Annie rounded a sharp curve and disappeared from sight.

Jack stood up on his pedals and pumped with all his might. He imagined Annie veering into the path of a vehicle or driving off the cliff!

When Jack finally came around the curve, he saw Annie up ahead, waiting beside the road. A big grin lit up her face. "Thank goodness, you're okay!" she called. "I was worried about you!"

Jack rode to her and stopped his bike.

"This road isn't safe, you know," said Annie.

"You're telling *me*?" said Jack, panting.

"But I can understand how that dragon felt. Can't you?" said Annie. "It's so beautiful!"

Jack caught his breath and looked around. "Yeah, it is," he said. "But how much farther do we have to go? We can't forget about our mission."

"I don't think it's much farther. Come on, we'll hurry," said Annie. She climbed back onto her bike.

"I'll go first," said Jack. "Let's stay together and keep as close as we can to the side of the road. I'm serious, Annie." He gripped his handlebars and started pedaling again.

Leading the way, Jack hugged the side of the road. He glanced back a couple of times to make sure Annie was doing the same. As they struggled uphill, huffing and puffing, a light rain started to fall. Mist gradually descended over the valley and the highway as they biked higher and higher up the mountain.

More vehicles roared by, but Jack tried to ignore them. He couldn't believe they were biking up a mountain on a Chinese highway in foggy weather!

Finally Jack and Annie came to a sign that said:

CONSERVATION AND RESEARCH CENTER FOR THE GIANT PANDA

"Yay! We're here!" said Annie.

The rain had stopped. Jack was wet, exhausted, and out of breath. "I hope you're—you're happy," he said.

Annie gave Jack a big smile. "I am," she said. "Totally."

The panda center was nestled between two tall mountains. It was on the far side of a narrow river. A small bridge crossed the river to the entrance gate. Near the gate a group of grown-ups was waiting to go inside.

Jack and Annie rode to the parking lot and parked their bikes next to a small blue bus. They took off their helmets and hung them from their handlebars.

"Oh, no!" cried Annie. She pointed to the panda center sign. At the bottom it said:

NO ONE UNDER 18 ADMITTED UNLESS ACCOMPANIED BY AN ADULT.

"I don't believe it," said Jack. "We came all this way for nothing?" He had to admit he was secretly relieved. Now they could get back to their mission.

"I can't accept this," said Annie. "We *have* to get in there."

"Your attention, please, everyone!" a woman in a uniform called to the group waiting outside the gate.

"Let's go listen," said Annie. She ran across the bridge.

"Annie!" Jack called. He sighed, and then hurried after her. They stood at the back of the little crowd.

"My name is Dr. Ling," the young Chinese woman said to the group. "Welcome to the largest giant panda reserve in the world. This is a place for scientists and animal protectors."

"That's me," Annie said, "animal protector."

Several people looked at Annie, as if they were wondering who she was.

Oh, brother, thought Jack.

"Good," Dr. Ling said to Annie. "Pandas are one of the most endangered species in the world. For at least three million years, they have lived in China's dense bamboo forests. Now those same forests are being cut down to make room for farms and roads."

"How many pandas are left?" asked Annie.

"Throughout the world, only about sixteen hundred in the wild," said Dr. Ling. "Today the species is threatened with extinction."

"That's terrible!" Annie said.

"Shhh," said Jack.

But Annie didn't *shhh*. "Can we save them, Dr. Ling?" she asked.

"We hope so. We're working hard to do just that at the panda center," said Dr. Ling. "We are responsible for about two hundred pandas here.

Many were rescued after an injury or illness. And many more were born here. Last year we had sixteen new babies."

"Wow!" said Annie.

"While the panda center is not a place for tourists," said Dr. Ling, "we *do* allow volunteers to come in and help us. So without further ado, let's all get suited up!"

Annie started walking with the crowd. "Annie, come back," Jack whispered loudly.

But Annie just signaled to Jack to follow her. Then she stepped boldly into the Conservation and Research Center for the Giant Panda.

CHAPTER FOUR

Get Suited Up!

"**I** don't believe her!" Jack grumbled to himself. He had no choice but to follow Annie into the panda center. When he walked through the gate, he saw a group of low buildings with tree-covered mountains looming behind them.

As Dr. Ling led the group along a stone path, Jack saw Annie talking to an elegant older woman with snow-white hair. He quickly caught up with them. He pulled on Annie's sleeve, but she kept talking to the woman. "I've *always* loved them," Annie said. "You too?"

"My goodness, yes," the woman said. "I've come all by myself from New York City to see them."

"That's great," said Annie. "We've come all the way from Pennsylvania! What's your name?"

"Sylvia," the woman answered. "And yours?"

"I'm Annie. This is my brother, Jack. Do you mind if we tag along with you, Sylvia?" said Annie.

"Of course not," said Sylvia. "I'd be delighted."

"Great." Annie smiled at Jack.

Dr. Ling led the group into one of the buildings and gave each person canvas coveralls, paper shoes, and rubber gloves. "All volunteers must wear these over their clothes," she said. "That way, we'll know you're here to help us."

"We're going to get caught," Jack whispered to Annie.

"Don't worry," she said. "We actually *are* with an adult now."

Jack shook his head. But he took off his pack, and he and Annie each pulled on large, bulky coveralls. They rolled up their sleeves and pant legs. Then they slid the paper shoes over their sneakers and tugged on the rubber gloves.

"We'll all go into the nursery first," said Dr. Ling.

Annie grabbed Jack's arm. She looked like she might explode with happiness.

Dr. Ling opened a door at the back of the room and herded everyone into the panda nursery. "We have only one newborn panda cub now. As you walk by the incubator, take a quick peek."

The group paraded slowly past the incubator. Almost everyone who peeked at the baby murmured with surprise. Jack quickly found out why—the newborn didn't look like a panda at all. It looked more like a fuzzy pink mouse.

"Incredible," said Jack.

"It's so teeny!" whispered Annie.

"Yes," Sylvia whispered back. "I've read that newborn pandas weigh less than half a pound. But they can grow into two-hundred-and-fifty-pound bears."

"Whoa," whispered Jack. He and Annie walked with Sylvia out of the nursery.

"Now let's go meet some of our panda keepers!" said Dr. Ling. She led the group over a stone walkway beside bamboo woods. Near a goldfish pond, several men in blue coveralls were waiting for them.

"These gentlemen are the panda keepers," said Dr. Ling. "You volunteers will work in pairs in the different panda houses. Each pair will spend a little time helping take care of a panda." She pointed to Jack and Annie. "You two go with Master Lee. He's

Bing-Bing's keeper. He'll take you to her house. I hope your grandmother doesn't mind."

Sylvia smiled. "Oh! I'm not—" she started to say.

"Bye, Grandma!" Annie said with a laugh.

Sylvia laughed, too, as if she thought Annie was making a joke, and she waved good-bye.

"See you later!" Annie called. Then she grabbed Jack by the arm again and pulled him along after Master Lee.

Master Lee was quiet and very serious-looking. Without a word, he led Jack and Annie to Bing-Bing's house. The panda's house was a giant cage with a door that opened into a yard. The yard was surrounded by a rock wall.

"Bing-Bing lives by herself here," Master Lee said. "She is an eight-year-old adult who joined us when she was quite small."

When they entered the cage, Jack saw leaves and bamboo stalks scattered across the concrete floor. But there was no panda inside.

"Where's Bing-Bing now?" said Annie.

"Somewhere in her yard," said Master Lee.

He grabbed two brooms from the corner.

Jack and Annie looked through the bars at the yard. They saw trees and bushes, but no sign of a giant panda.

"She must have found a good hiding place," said Annie.

"Yes. I do not think you will see her today," Master Lee said matter-of-factly.

"Oh, no," said Annie.

"Can we look for her?" asked Jack.

"No, Bing-Bing is very shy. We have to respect that," said Master Lee. "I am going to get fresh bamboo now. You can clean her house by removing yesterday's uneaten bamboo stalks and sweeping the floor." He handed brooms to Jack and Annie.

"Is bamboo Bing-Bing's favorite food?" asked Jack.

"Yes, *all* pandas eat bamboo for breakfast, lunch, and dinner," said Master Lee.

"Wow, they must really love it," said Annie.

"Can humans eat bamboo, too?" Jack asked.

"If they tried, they would break their teeth,"

Master Lee answered without smiling. "Only a creature with superstrong jaws can eat bamboo."

"So it's very tough," said Jack, growing excited. "Is it as tough as *wood*?"

"Well, yes . . . ," said Master Lee.

"And I'll bet it's really healthy, too!" said Annie.

"Uh, no . . . ," said Master Lee. "Bamboo is *not* very nutritious. That's why a panda must eat a lot of it. Some pandas at the center eat eighty pounds a day."

"Oh, okay," said Annie, her shoulders sagging. "And I guess it's not baked with love, either. Is it?"

Master Lee stared at Annie. He looked confused. "No . . . of course not," he said.

"Darn," said Annie.

Jack was embarrassed. *Like the waiter in the restaurant, Master Lee must think we're really weird,* he thought.

"Well!" said Master Lee. "Shall we get to work now?"

"Sure," said Annie.

"Sweep up the stalks, as well as the panda waste," said Master Lee. "Then discard everything there." He pointed to a trash bin in the cage.

"Panda waste?" said Jack.

"Yes," said Master Lee. Seeing Jack's expression, he added, "It's not bad, I promise you. Their droppings look like little dry straw baskets."

Jack looked around. He saw what he thought Master Lee was talking about. It didn't look that bad.

"I will be back," said Master Lee. "I am going to get fresh bamboo from the farmer's truck." Master Lee then left through the door at the back of the cage.

"Darn," said Jack, "we struck out."

"No special food here," said Annie. She looked out in the yard. "And no panda here, either. I really want to see Bing-Bing!"

"How did this happen?" said Jack. "We should be working on our mission. Not stuck in a cage picking up panda poop."

Annie giggled. "Don't worry, we'll leave soon," she said. "Let's just do our job first. It's nice to help out here."

"Yeah, sure," said Jack. "Sweep fast."

Jack and Annie began sweeping up old bamboo stalks and panda droppings. Jack filled a dustpan. As he dumped everything into the trash bin, Annie gasped.

"I see her!" she whispered. "She's up in a tree!"

CHAPTER FIVE

Bing-Bing

Annie pulled Jack to the bars of the panda house and pointed out to the yard. "See? Over there," she whispered.

A giant panda was climbing down the trunk of a maple tree, rump-first. She touched the ground, then sat up and raised her head. She was bigger than Jack had expected. Her head was the size of a basketball.

"Oh, wow!" said Annie. "She's amazing!"

"Yeah, she is," whispered Jack.

The giant panda was much more amazing in

real life than in photos, Jack thought. She looked like a gigantic stuffed animal that had come alive. Her nostrils quivered as she sniffed the air. Her black ears twitched.

"Hello, Bing-Bing," Master Lee said.

Jack and Annie jumped in surprise.

Master Lee pushed a cart loaded with bamboo through the back door of the cage.

"Can we go out in the yard and pet Bing-Bing?" asked Annie.

"Oh, no," said Master Lee. "We always keep our big pandas separated from our visitors. They won't hurt you, but we don't want people intruding on their space."

"Really?" said Annie.

"Pandas are not pets," said Master Lee. "They are wild animals. We want them to live as naturally as possible."

"That makes sense . . . ," said Annie. She let out a big sigh as she stared at Bing-Bing. "It's just that she looks so soft and cuddly."

Jack felt sorry for Annie. He knew how

badly she wanted to be close to the panda. "At least we get to actually *see* one," he said.

"Now that we have found Bing-Bing, I have one more job for you," said Master Lee. He handed each of them clipboards with paper and pencils. "I need you to record data. If she stays in view, observe her and write down every sound and movement she makes. Can you do that?"

"Sure. Jack loves to collect data," said Annie, trying to be cheerful. "And I love to watch animals."

"So you are true scientists. Good," said Master Lee. "Now I will get more bamboo." The panda keeper dumped the cartful of bamboo onto the floor, then left Jack and Annie alone.

Jack and Annie took off their gloves and observed Bing-Bing through the bars. They held their pencils, ready to record data.

The giant panda didn't pay any attention to them. She sat against the maple tree and scratched her back by rubbing it up and down the trunk. Then she scratched the top of her head with a forepaw and her belly with a hind paw.

Annie giggled. Jack wrote:

scratches back, head, and belly

The panda raised a paw and scratched her nose. Jack added:

and nose

The panda swatted at a fly to shoo it away. Jack wrote:

swats fly

"Hey, I think she's coming over here!" Annie whispered.

Bing-Bing had stood up. She was staring in Jack and Annie's direction. Then she started moving on all fours with graceful rolling steps. She came right up to the bars of the cage, sat down, and peered at Jack and Annie.

Jack held his breath. He felt as if he and Annie were zoo animals and the panda was a curious visitor observing them.

The giant panda tilted her large head. Then she covered her eyes with her paws.

"Oh my gosh!" Annie whispered with delight.

The panda put her paws down and looked directly at Jack. He stared back into her bright, intelligent eyes. Holding her gaze, he lowered his pencil and clipboard.

Jack felt as if he were falling through time. For a moment, the panda wasn't eight years old. She was three million years old. She was filled with wisdom. She knew things he could never understand. He didn't know what to write—words couldn't possibly capture the wonder of her.

"I'm back. How are you doing?" asked Master Lee.

Jack snapped out of his dreamlike thoughts and turned to the panda keeper. "Uh . . . fine," he said.

"How unusual that Bing-Bing came so close to

you," said Master Lee, walking over to them. "Did you record her behavior?"

Silently, Jack and Annie handed him their pencils and clipboards. Annie's paper was blank, and only a few words were written on Jack's.

"Ah," said Master Lee with a smile. "Well, if you ever come back, you can observe more."

Jack nodded, but he knew he'd observed a lot—only it was more with his heart than his head.

"You have to go now," said Master Lee. "I saw your grandmother headed to the bus with everyone else. I'm surprised she didn't come for you."

"She's a little forgetful sometimes," said Annie. She turned back to the panda, who was still staring at them. "Bye, Bing-Bing."

"Bye, Bing-Bing," Jack murmured, looking into the panda's eyes once again. He hated to leave. Their time together had been too short.

"Hurry," said Master Lee. "You don't want to keep the others waiting."

Master Lee ushered them out the back door

of the cage and along the path. He stopped at the goldfish pond. "Follow the stone path to the entrance gate. Don't forget to leave your volunteer clothes in one of the bins there."

"Thank you, Master Lee," said Jack.

"Good-bye," said Master Lee. Then he turned and headed back to Bing-Bing's house.

"I have to admit, that was really, really great," said Jack. "Ready to get back to our mission now?"

"Yes," said Annie, "but first, let's follow the path the other way. Maybe we can get a quick peek at some more pandas."

"Okay, but a *really* quick peek," said Jack. "We have to solve that riddle."

Jack and Annie started down the path that led away from the main entrance. They went around a corner and stopped. "Oh, wow!" they said together, and then they burst into laughter.

A dozen little panda cubs were playing in a huge fenced-in area. A sign said:

PANDA KINDERGARTEN

The cubs were the size of chubby human toddlers. Some were swinging on rubber tires and wooden swing sets. Others were climbing logs or sliding down a slide. Some rolled in the grass, while others wrestled, tumbled, or did somersaults.

"Oh! Oh! Oh! I *love* them!" said Annie. "They *all* look just like Roly and Poly! I love them *so much,* don't you?"

"Yeah, I do. They're really cute," said Jack, laughing. "Look at those guys on the—"

"Hey, what are you two still doing here?" someone said.

Jack and Annie turned in surprise.

Dr. Ling was hurrying down the path toward them. "Everyone has left! Your grandmother and the rest of the group must have forgotten all about you! How irresponsible! Go! Go! Try to catch them!"

"Grandma!" cried Annie. She and Jack took off running. Laughing, they tore to the front entrance. They yanked off their volunteer clothes and shoes and threw them into a bin by the gate. Then they dashed across the bridge.

The tour bus was turning onto the highway as Jack and Annie charged into the parking lot.

"Bye, Grandma!" yelled Annie, waving.

Jack laughed. "Come on," he said. "Let's grab our bikes and go—before Sylvia gets in trouble."

Jack and Annie were both laughing as they

climbed on their mountain bikes and started back toward Wolong Town.

The sun had come out from behind the clouds. It made the wet green fields in the valley sparkle. Not only was it a beautiful ride, Jack thought, but pedaling back to the town was a lot easier than pedaling uphill to the panda center. For a little while, he was able to coast without pedaling at all.

"I hated to leave the pandas!" Annie shouted.

"Me too!" Jack yelled back. "I loved Bing-Bing and the cubs and the newborn baby! But the sooner we get back to Wolong Town, the sooner we can help save Penny! What time do you think it is?"

"I saw a clock near the center's entrance," said Annie. "It said two-fifteen. That still gives us lots of time."

"Good!" said Jack.

"Where will we look for that healthy, tough, round food?" said Annie.

"I guess we need to visit more restaurants," yelled Jack.

"Yes!" said Annie. "I'm starving!"

"Me too!" said Jack. "Bring on the green bean jelly and fried stinky tofu!"

Annie laughed. She yelled something back, but Jack didn't hear her. "What did you say?" he called.

Before Annie could answer, a deep rumbling sound filled the air. Then the roadway trembled and buckled, and everything around them—bushes, rocks, and trees—began shaking and moving.

CHAPTER SIX

The Dragon Wakes

Jack put on his brakes and jumped off his bike. Annie did the same. A huge boulder crashed down the mountain slope beside them. The boulder slammed onto the road right in front of them. They looked around wildly. Rocks were sliding and tumbling. Trees were whipping back and forth and then breaking apart. Branches, rocks, and dirt cascaded down the slope.

As Jack tried to figure out what to do, another boulder tumbled down—and then another! Jack pulled Annie off the road. They scrambled into a rocky crevice and huddled down. Clods of dirt hit their bike helmets.

The ground finally stopped shaking and rumbling. For a moment, neither Jack nor Annie said anything. Then Jack uttered one word: *"Earthquake."*

"I know," Annie said hoarsely. "Like—like that earthquake we lived through in San Francisco."

"Except there, *buildings* crumbled around us," said Jack. "Here, it's mountains."

"I think it's stopped," said Annie. "Let's look."

Annie started to stand up, but Jack pulled her back down. "Wait!" The ground had started shaking again. "Aftershock!" he said. "Watch out—more stuff might fall."

No sooner had Jack said that than another enormous boulder crashed to the ground. Then another one tumbled down. The earth stopped trembling again, but the air was so thick with dust and grit that it made Jack's eyes burn.

"I wonder if the pandas are all right," said Annie.

"Oh, man!" said Jack. "Bing-Bing!" He pictured the giant panda in her yard, trapped under a rock or a tree!

"We've got to go back!" said Annie.

"I know!" said Jack. They both scrambled out to the road. "Where are our bikes?"

Jack and Annie looked around. As the dust settled, they saw massive damage up and down the highway. Fallen rocks, mud, and trees blocked both the way to Wolong Town and the way back to the panda center. A boulder the size of a car had crushed both their bikes.

Jack and Annie took off their helmets and dropped them to the ground. "We can't go back to the panda center now," said Annie. "We can't go to town. We can't go anywhere."

"No kidding," said Jack. "You'd have to be King Kong to get over this stuff."

"King Kong," Annie repeated. Then she looked at Jack and grinned.

"What?" he said.

"King Kong. No problem," she said. "We can do it."

"Do what?" said Jack.

"Turn into King Kongs!" said Annie. "Well, not quite as big as King Kong, maybe, but we could be five times bigger than we are now."

"Ohhhh," said Jack. He'd forgotten all about their magic potion!

"It's perfect," said Annie. "It's the only way we can get out of here."

"Yeah . . . ," said Jack, letting out a long breath. He reached into his backpack and took out the small bottle that held the potion.

"Five times our size," said Annie. "You're almost five feet tall. So you'll be almost twenty-five feet tall. And I'll be just a little shorter."

"Right," said Jack.

"But we can only use it once," said Annie. "And we only have an hour. *And* we have to choose which way to go: back to Wolong Town or back to the panda center. If we go to town, we can keep looking for the special food to save Penny—if the restaurants are still standing."

"Plus we can leave in the tree house whenever we're ready," said Jack.

"Right," said Annie. "But we'd have to leave Bing-Bing and the rest of the pandas behind. And we wouldn't know what happened to them, and we wouldn't be able to help."

Jack stared at the bottle. It was a terrible choice. Then he thought of something. "Remember on our last mission, you said that when we do the right thing, it feels like it somehow helps Penny—even if it seems to take us *away* from our goal?"

Annie smiled. "Yep, and everything worked out on that mission, didn't it?"

Jack nodded.

"Panda center!" they said together.

"You take a sip first," said Annie.

Jack popped the tiny cork out of the bottle. He tilted his head back and took a quick sip. He licked his lips, then held the bottle out to Annie.

Just as Annie took the bottle from Jack, the ground trembled with another aftershock.

Jack started to shake.

"Yikes!" cried Annie.

The aftershock ended, and the ground stopped trembling. But Jack kept shaking.

Annie yelled something, but Jack couldn't understand what she was saying. His body was still quaking. He had started to grow!

CHAPTER SEVEN

Jack the Giant

Jack felt as if someone was gripping his head—
and pulling him up, and up, and up! He looked
down and watched his arms and hands stretch out.
His legs grew longer, his feet bigger.

Jack rocked back and forth, then stood still. He
had stopped stretching and growing. His shoes,
clothes, and backpack had all grown bigger to fit
his new body.

"Jack!" Annie's voice sounded distant.

Peering through the dust, Jack looked around
for Annie.

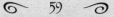

"Jack! Down here!"

Jack looked down. Annie was standing next to him. She only came up to his knees! "I dropped the bottle and it broke!" she said. "I didn't get to drink the potion!"

"Oh, no!" Jack boomed. Even his voice was bigger. "I'm so sorry."

"You're huge!" said Annie. "How does it feel? Is it fun?"

"Not yet," said Jack.

The earth trembled again with another after-shock. Annie lost her balance and fell. Jack leaned over and picked her up with both hands. He placed her on one of his giant shoulders.

"Whoa," said Annie. "This is cool! Now I'm taller than *you*! I can be your lookout."

From their new height, Jack and Annie could see over the rubble to the vast devastation. Trees down in the valley had been uprooted. The river was wild and raging. The mountaintops were shrouded in dark clouds.

"It's starting to rain again," said Annie.

"That's the least of our problems," said Jack. "I just hope the earthquake didn't destroy the panda center."

"I know! Let's hurry! We only have an hour!" said Annie.

Annie held on to Jack's head, and Jack held on to Annie's legs. He lifted one giant foot and stepped over the boulder that had crushed their bikes. Picking his way through the rubble, he headed back to the panda center. He stepped over fallen debris, power lines, and deep cracks in the road. His enormous sneakers crushed twigs and brush.

Jack stepped over huge mounds of mud as if they were anthills. He kicked away boulders as if they were soccer balls. He tossed aside fallen trees as if they were broken branches. He leapt over a river of water coursing down from the mountain as if it were a rain puddle.

"This is incredible!" said Jack.

"Watch out!" said Annie. A boulder was rolling down the wet road toward them.

Jack spread his legs wide, and the boulder went between them and kept rolling downhill.

Jack and Annie laughed. "*Now* are you having fun?" she said.

Jack nodded. "Maybe a little bit."

Suddenly a tree crashed across the road. Jack stumbled over it. He fell to the ground just as a wall of mud came cascading down the mountain slope. The black ooze was filled with rock fragments and plants.

Annie! thought Jack. He lifted his head out of the mud before it smothered him. He reached around and felt Annie's kicking feet. He pulled her out of the thick, wet goo.

"You okay?" Jack shouted.

"Yes!" sputtered Annie. "But we're sliding over the cliff!"

Annie was right. With the force of a tidal wave, the mudslide was pushing them across the highway toward the cliff!

Jack clutched Annie under one of his huge arms. Then he struggled through the grimy ooze until they were clear of the mudslide. Covered with mud from his hair to his shoes, Jack felt heavy and uncomfortable. He even had mud in his mouth. He put Annie down and sat on the road.

"At least we're—we're safe," Annie said.

Jack coughed, gagging on mud.

"You look like a giant swamp monster," Annie said.

Jack couldn't talk. As the rain fell harder, he threw back his head and let rainwater wash his face and fill his mouth. He choked and spit and coughed until his throat was clear. With help from the pelting rain, he washed the mud off his bare arms and his shirt, jeans, and sneakers. Finally he looked at Annie.

"How long do you think I've been a giant now?" he asked hoarsely.

"I don't know," she said. "It seems like a long time."

"We'd better get moving. We only have an hour," he said.

"What'll we do if you're still a giant when we get to the center?" asked Annie.

"I'll hide outside," said Jack, "until I'm small again." He figured the last thing the staff needed now was to see a twenty-five-foot-tall kid.

Slowly they both stood up, soaking wet, but cleaner. Jack lifted Annie back onto his shoulder. He began striding uphill again, sloshing through mud puddles and stepping over crushed rocks. Jack walked through the falling rain, never stopping. But by the time they reached the panda center, he was so tired he could barely take another step.

With Annie on his shoulder, Jack stood on the bank of the river and they stared across at the damage wrought by the earthquake.

The parking lot was filled with mud. The center's sign had been knocked down. Portions of the bridge had collapsed into the river, and fallen brush and debris were piled up on the other side of the entrance gate.

The slopes that surrounded the center were now gray and bare. Landslides had stripped them of foliage.

"If it's this bad outside the center," said Jack, "I wonder how bad it is inside."

"How do we even *get* inside?" said Annie, staring down at the raging river.

"Don't worry," said Jack. "I'm pretty sure I'm tall enough to wade across." He took a deep breath, then stepped into the river. The cold water swirled around his waist. The current nearly knocked him

over. Slowly and carefully, he stepped around a huge rock that had rolled into the river. Suddenly Jack felt his body start to quake.

Another aftershock, he thought. He paused, but his body kept shaking. As Jack shook, he started to grow smaller. In an instant he had shrunk back to his normal size.

He and Annie plunged into the swiftly churning water. Jack grabbed the branch of a fallen tree. Clinging to the branch, he looked around frantically for Annie. She was holding on to a log. "Here!" shrieked Jack. He reached out his hand, and Annie grabbed it. As the water swirled around them, he pulled her over to him.

"Can we get to the bridge?" Annie cried.

"Try!" yelled Jack. They both let go of the branch and thrashed through the water until they grabbed on to a piece of the wrecked bridge.

Jack and Annie hoisted themselves up onto the slab of concrete. Jack pointed to the part of the bridge that still stood at the edge of the ravine. He took another deep breath and leapt over the gap onto the broken bridge. Annie followed.

Jack and Annie clung to a piece of bridge railing and stared at the entrance gate of the panda center. Muddy rocks, branches, and leaves were piled on the other side.

"I think we can climb over," said Annie. She led the way, stepping onto the railing next to the gate.

Jack followed her. They climbed over the gate and kept climbing over the heap of branches, brush, and rocks that blocked the entrance. When they reached the top of the wreckage, they looked down.

Staff members were rushing around with buckets, shovels, and first-aid kits. When Master Lee and Dr. Ling caught sight of Jack and Annie, they both stopped dead in their tracks and gaped at them.

"Hi there," Annie called. "Can we help?"

CHAPTER EIGHT

One Panda at a Time

"**Y**es, thank you! We need all the help we can get," said Dr. Ling. She looked dazed and frightened.

Jack and Annie scrambled down from the wreckage.

"Where's your grandmother?" asked Dr. Ling.

"Um . . . she's . . ." Jack looked at Annie.

"Helping earthquake victims south of here," said Annie.

"Good for her," said Dr. Ling, sighing. "Everyone needs help."

"This is a huge disaster for our region," said

Master Lee. "We have no water or electricity. We've been able to make calls on cell phones, but we must conserve the batteries."

"How's Bing-Bing?" Jack asked.

"She's missing," said Master Lee. His voice quavered.

"Missing?" said Jack.

"Yes," said Master Lee. "I can't find her anywhere."

"Don't worry, we'll help you!" said Annie.

Master Lee's eyes welled with tears. "Thank you," he said. "She is like a member of my family." He took a deep breath, then spoke clearly and steadily. "The pandas are terrified by the quake and the landslides. Many of their homes have been destroyed. The stone walls around their yards have collapsed."

"We also have staff who have been injured," said Dr. Ling. "Master Lee and I must go now to help those who have been trapped in the rubble."

"While you do that, we'll look for Bing-Bing," said Annie.

"Thank you," said Master Lee again, "but be very careful. Remember, she's a wild animal. She might be so upset and confused that she could attack you by mistake."

"We'll remember. Come on, Jack!" said Annie.

"Oh, wait," said Dr. Ling. "So everyone will know you are here to help, please put your volunteer clothes back on." She pointed to the bin, then she and Master Lee hurried off.

Jack and Annie grabbed their coveralls from the bin and pulled them on over their wet clothes. "Let's check around Bing-Bing's house first," said Jack.

He and Annie ran across the grounds over shards of glass and fallen debris. They passed broken windows and cracked concrete walls. The kindergarten area was empty of cubs. The quake had overturned the swing sets and slide.

When Jack and Annie arrived at Bing-Bing's house, they saw that the stone wall enclosing her yard had crumbled.

"She must have run off into the woods," said Jack.

"We have to go look for her," said Annie.

Jack and Annie climbed over the collapsed wall. Then they scrambled over piles of shrubs and branches into the forest.

"Bing-Bing!" Annie called.

"Bing-Bing!" Jack echoed.

They kept moving through the broken brush until Jack stopped. He grabbed Annie. "Shhh!" he said, and pointed.

Bing-Bing was sitting in the middle of a fallen bamboo grove. Her forepaws rested in her lap. Her head sagged on her chest, and her eyes were closed. The giant panda was snoring.

"She looks exhausted," said Jack.

Annie smiled. "She doesn't look like she's going to attack us," she said.

Bing-Bing raised her head. When she saw Jack and Annie, she let out a bellow.

"Don't be scared, Bing-Bing," said Jack.

He and Annie crept closer to the panda. They knelt down beside her.

"Hi there," said Annie. She gently patted the giant panda's furry head.

Bing-Bing made soft sounds.

"Are you hungry?" asked Jack. He picked up a broken bamboo stalk and offered it to the panda. She took the shoot in her paws and pulled off the leaves with her teeth. She gazed at Jack as she chewed. He thought she looked weary and sad.

"Listen," Annie whispered.

Soft whimpering sounds came from the trees beyond the thicket.

Annie stood up and quietly stepped through the broken bamboo. "Look! It's Roly and Poly!" she said.

"Wait here," Jack said to Bing-Bing. "Keep eating." He hurried to Annie's side. High up in a tree were two small pandas.

"It's okay, it's okay," said Jack, as if he were talking to little children. "Come down now. One panda at a time."

"Come on, Roly." Annie coaxed the nearest panda cub. "Come to me."

The small panda started down the tree trunk, rump-first. When he got close to the ground,

Annie put her arms around him and pried him loose from the tree. Roly made little chirping sounds.

"I understand," Annie said to the cub. "The earthquake was awful, wasn't it? You were so scared, but you're fine now. I've got you."

"You're next, Poly!" said Jack. "Come down!"

Poly hugged the trunk and used the soles of her feet to pull herself up even higher into the tree.

"Not *up!*" called Jack. *"Down!"*

As the little panda looked down at him, her hind paws slipped on the trunk. With a shriek, she tumbled to the ground.

Jack dropped to his knees and put his arms around Poly. "Don't worry, I've got you," he said, cuddling her. "You're safe now."

The panda nibbled Jack's arm with soft, tiny bites. Jack laughed. "That tickles," he said.

"We have to get them back to the center," said Annie.

Jack stood up and lifted Poly into his arms. The cub was surprisingly heavy! "Come with us, Bing-Bing!" he called to the giant panda. She was still chewing her bamboo stem.

"Lead us back to Master Lee, Bing-Bing!" said Annie. "He misses you!"

Bing-Bing licked her paws. She stood on all fours and shook herself like a dog. Then she started toward the panda center with her rolling gait.

Jack and Annie carried the cubs through the brush, until more whimpering panda sounds made them stop.

"Wait, Bing-Bing!" called Jack.

"Look!" said Annie.

A third cub—smaller than the other two—was peeking out from behind an old tree stump.

"Hi there!" said Jack.

The cub rushed toward Jack, yipping like a puppy. He clasped Jack's legs and held on tightly. Clutching Poly gently under his right arm, Jack bent down and put his left arm around the little panda. The frightened cub was shivering. "Poor little guy," said Jack.

"Can you carry Little Guy, too?" asked Annie.

"I'll try," said Jack. He clumsily scooped Little Guy off the ground.

"Got him?" said Annie.

"Yep." Jack felt as if he were carrying two

chubby little kids—except these kids had fur and paws! "All set," he said. "Let's go, gang!"

Jack held on tightly to Little Guy and Poly. Annie carried Roly in her arms. Bing-Bing trotted ahead over the fallen rocks and crushed bamboo. They all climbed over the ruins of the collapsed wall.

Master Lee was standing in Bing-Bing's yard. When he saw the panda, his face lit up. "Bing!" he cried, and raced across the yard toward her.

Bing-Bing sat on her back legs, and Master Lee grabbed her forepaws. "Oh, Bing! You're not hurt one bit, are you?" he said. He hugged the giant panda and laughed.

Bing-Bing made snorting noises that sounded like laughter, too.

Dr. Ling came running into the yard. "The missing cubs!" she cried. "Where did you find them?"

"Hiding in the trees," said Annie.

The cubs made screeching sounds, as if they were trying to tell Dr. Ling about their terrifying adventure.

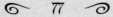

Dr. Ling smiled. "We'll take them to the nursery and give them milk to calm them down," she said. "We're using a small generator to keep the incubator going for the newborn."

"Did you help everyone out of the rubble?" Annie asked her.

"Yes. All the workers at the panda center are safe now," said Dr. Ling, "just bruised and shaken. We are very fortunate, for we have word that other workers in the nature reserve are harmed or missing. Let us go."

Before he went with Dr. Ling, Jack looked back. He saw Master Lee dancing with Bing-Bing, holding her paws and rocking from side to side. "See you later, guys!" Jack called. Then he followed Annie to the panda nursery.

Inside, the tiny newborn panda was safe in her incubator. At least ten small pandas were lying on their backs on a blanket on the floor. They were all drinking milk from baby bottles.

"Aww! That's the cutest thing I've ever seen!" cried Annie.

Dr. Ling brought bottles for Roly, Poly, and Little Guy. The three cubs held their bottles with their forepaws. "We put a little sedative in the milk to help them go to sleep," said Dr. Ling.

As the cubs sucked on the bottles, a roaring sound filled the air. For a moment, Jack thought the noise was from another aftershock, but Dr. Ling smiled. "Ah, good," she said. "The helicopter has arrived."

CHAPTER NINE

Totally All Right

"Helicopter?" said Jack.

"Yes, I received a call on my cell phone from the military," said Dr. Ling. "They're bringing medical supplies and food."

"That's great," said Annie.

"We need to get our pandas to other reserves," said Dr. Ling. "Until the road is cleared, we will send some by helicopter to Wolong Town. From there, a van will take them to a safe reserve."

"That sounds like a good plan," said Jack.

Dr. Ling smiled. "I am glad you think so,

because I would like to ask you to accompany these three cubs on their first helicopter flight. Do you think your grandmother would mind?"

"No problem. We've been in choppers before," Annie said casually. "Antarctica."

"Really?" said Dr. Ling. She looked surprised. "Well, good. I'll be right back. I need to speak to the helicopter pilot and make a quick call to our staff in Wolong Town."

Dr. Ling started to leave the nursery, then stopped. "Why, I just realized—I don't even know your names," she said.

"Jack and Annie," said Annie.

Dr. Ling nodded. "Thanks, Jack and Annie," she said, and then left.

"This is so cool," Jack said to Annie. "I was wondering how we'd get back to Wolong Town and complete our mission."

Annie smiled at Jack. "Remember—things always seem to work out when we just do the next right thing," she said.

"Funny how that works," said Jack.

"And this way, we won't have to leave the cubs yet," said Annie. She wiped milk off Roly's mouth with her hand and kissed the top of his head. All three cubs had dropped their bottles and were nodding off to sleep.

"Can you stay with the kids while I say good-bye to Bing-Bing?" said Jack.

"Sure," said Annie. "Say good-bye for me, too."

"I will." Jack hurried out the door. He dashed along the path to Bing-Bing's house, sidestepping rubble and glass.

Jack found Master Lee sitting with Bing-Bing on the concrete floor. He was quietly feeding her bits of bread from a small, round loaf. For a moment, the earthquake disaster seemed far away.

"Bing-Bing loves a snack," Master Lee said, smiling at the panda, "even when the world is turned upside down."

"I know," said Jack, kneeling beside them. "I gave her some bamboo in the woods. What's she eating now?"

"It's a special treat," said Master Lee. "Here. You can give it to her." He handed Jack the loaf.

The bread was very hard. Jack struggled to break off a piece. Bing-Bing opened her mouth wide, and Jack placed the bread on her pink tongue. As the giant panda chewed, she stared at Jack with her wise and gentle gaze.

"I thought she ate bamboo," said Jack.

"She does," said Master Lee. "This *is* bamboo, but it's ground up and mixed with molasses, grains, and vitamins. It's very healthy. We call it panda bread."

Jack turned his head to look at Master Lee. "And it's baked with love?" he said.

"Yes . . . ," said Master Lee, looking puzzled.

Jack gave him a radiant smile.

"Is everything all right?" asked Master Lee.

"Yes. Everything's all right," said Jack. "Totally all right."

"Good . . . I'm glad," said Master Lee. "It has been a very difficult day."

"It has," agreed Jack. "Annie and I have to take the cubs to Wolong Town, in a helicopter. Would it be okay if I took a little panda bread with me? To show Annie?"

"Yes, certainly," said Master Lee. He gave Jack a small hunk of the panda bread. "But don't try to eat it," he said. "It's very—"

"Tough," finished Jack. "I know—tough as wood." He put the bread in his backpack. Then he stroked Bing-Bing's fur. "Bye, beautiful," he said. He turned to Master Lee. "Bing-Bing is really lucky to have you in her family, Master Lee."

The panda keeper nodded shyly. "Thank you," he said.

Jack and the giant panda exchanged one last look, then Jack hurried outside.

Leaping over the rubble, Jack ran back to the nursery. On his way, he saw that the helicopter had landed on the kindergarten playground. Soldiers in green-and-tan uniforms were unloading boxes.

Jack found Dr. Ling and Annie waiting for him.

They were holding Roly and Poly. "Jack, if you take the smallest cub, I will help you all get settled in the helicopter," said Dr. Ling.

"Sure!" Jack picked up Little Guy. The cub was drowsy and cuddly.

"Let's go!" said Dr. Ling.

Dr. Ling, Jack, and Annie left the nursery and carried the little pandas outside. Night was falling as they stood in the playground and watched the soldiers finish unloading food and medicine.

"Until you can get *all* the pandas out of here, how will you take care of them?" asked Annie.

"We will set up tents and carry water from the stream and get by as best we can," said Dr. Ling. "I believe people here in China and around the world will help us. I've already had a call from Pandas International. They promised to send powdered milk for the young ones, and they will write about our situation and raise money to help the pandas."

"Cool," said Jack. "Hey, in that case . . ." He reached into his pocket and pulled out the rest of their money. "We'd like to give something for the pandas, too." He handed their Chinese currency to Dr. Ling.

"Thank you!" she said. "All of this province will need help in the days to come. I have heard from the staff in Chengdu that this has been one of the most damaging earthquakes of all time. They think many people have been killed. Whole towns have been destroyed."

"That's terrible," said Jack.

"What about *your* family?" said Annie.

"My parents are safe in Beijing," said Dr. Ling. "But in the face of this disaster, everyone in our nation is one big family now. Oh, look, the pilot is waving to us."

In the twilight, Jack, Annie, and Dr. Ling each carried a cub to the helicopter. They climbed up the steps and entered the small cabin. Jack and Annie sat down and buckled their seat belts. Dr. Ling handed Roly to Annie. Annie hugged Roly and Poly while Jack cradled Little Guy in his arms.

"You will need this," said Dr. Ling. She pulled a small flashlight from her pocket and gave it to Annie. "It will be dark when you arrive. Wolong Town is without power, too."

"Thanks," said Jack.

"When you land, staff members from our office in Wolong Town will be waiting for you," said Dr. Ling. "Have a safe trip, and thank you for everything. Good-bye, Jack and Annie."

"Good luck rebuilding the panda center," said Jack. "It's an amazing place."

Dr. Ling climbed out of the helicopter and waved. The military pilot hopped aboard. "The ride will be very noisy," he told Jack and Annie, putting headphones over their ears. Then he took his seat. The two soldiers sat behind him.

A moment later, the engine roared and the blades started to spin. The helicopter shook; then it lifted off the ground and buzzed away from the panda center, through the darkening sky.

CHAPTER TEN

Panda Bread

The helicopter flew over the broken bridge, over the blocked highway, and over the crumbling mountains of the Wolong Reserve. Soon it roared over Wolong Town.

The pilot landed in a large field lit by emergency spotlights. Two other helicopters were also in the field. Tents had been set up, and people were carrying the injured on stretchers to the helicopters.

When the blades completely stopped turning, Jack and Annie carried the sleeping cubs out of the cabin and down the steps to the field.

"Jack! Annie!" someone called. Four women dressed in dark coveralls rushed to greet them. "We work for the panda center. Thank you for bringing the cubs to us!" one said.

Annie kissed each of the little pandas. "Be good now," she said.

Then she and Jack handed them over to the women. "We really love them," said Annie.

"I am so glad," said one of the women. "We will get them to a safe new home very soon. Later the others will join them there."

"We must help you, too," said another woman. "Go with Mrs. Chang to our office, and she will locate your grandmother."

"Oh, that's okay . . . ," said Jack. "We know exactly where she is." He started to back up.

Annie did the same. "That's right," she said. She pointed to the street. "We're going to meet her in a restaurant in town."

"Good-bye," said Jack.

"Good-bye," said Annie.

Before any of the women could speak, Jack grabbed Annie's hand and started to run. They ran across the busy field, weaving around the tents and helicopters, doctors, nurses, and military people. When they came to the street, they stopped to catch their breath.

"Ready to go home?" asked Jack.

"No, wait," said Annie. "We still have to find the special food."

"No, actually, we don't," said Jack.

"What?" said Annie.

"I said we don't have to look for the special food anymore," said Jack.

"But why? What do you mean?" said Annie.

"We . . . don't . . . have . . . to . . . *look* . . . for . . . it," Jack said.

Annie stared at him. "Are you saying we *have* it?" she asked.

Jack nodded, then pulled the hunk of panda bread out of his backpack. "It's called panda bread! When I went to say good-bye to Bing-Bing, Master Lee was feeding it to her."

"But what makes you think—" began Annie.

Jack held up his hand, interrupting her. "Panda bread is a healthy food," he said. "It's grainy and good, baked with love, tough as wood, round in shape, and the color of sand. *And* it's given to those who have lost their land—the pandas at the center!"

"Perfect!" breathed Annie.

Jack held up the panda bread and looked at it. "This is why I think pandas will survive," he said.

"Why?" asked Annie. "Because of panda bread?"

"Nope," said Jack. He put the bread into his pack. "I think they'll survive because people take responsibility for them. People make healthy bread for them and carry them to safety and raise money for them. And people speak up for them because they can't speak up for themselves."

"That's it," said Annie. "That's what panda bread stands for! It stands for people protecting and saving animals."

"Exactly," said Jack. "And now we have to go save Penny."

"Great," said Annie. "I think the tree house is nearby." She looked around. "Yes! It's there, in that line of trees. See it?"

"Yep," said Jack. "Let's go!"

When they came to the grove of trees, Jack switched on their small flashlight. The beam of light guided them to the rope ladder hanging in the dark.

"Wait! Our volunteer clothes!" said Annie.

They took off their coveralls and left them at the bottom of the tree. Then they climbed up the rope ladder into the tree house.

"Is everything still here?" asked Annie.

Jack shined the flashlight into a corner of the tree house. The light fell on the emerald rose, the white and yellow flower, and the gray goose feather. "It's all here," he said.

"Add the fourth thing," said Annie.

Jack pulled out the panda bread from his backpack and placed it on the floor next to the feather.

"Good," said Annie.

Roaring sounds filled the night. Jack and Annie looked out the window and saw another helicopter coming in.

"Remember our helicopter ride in Antarctica?" said Annie. "When you hid Penny in your jacket?"

"I totally remember it," said Jack. "We couldn't let anyone see her and she kept peeping, so I had to keep pretending to cough." He thought about the penguin's big eyes and her fuzzy little head. He thought about Teddy and Kathleen and the wonder and beauty of Camelot. Suddenly he couldn't wait to be there and help bring Penny back to life. "Are you ready to go to Camelot?" he asked Annie.

"Absolutely!" she said.

Jack reached into his backpack again and took out their note from Teddy and Kathleen. He pointed to the word *Camelot*. "I wish we could go *there*," he said.

A blast of light—

a roar of wind—

a rumble of thunder—

and all was quiet.

CHAPTER ELEVEN

Breaking the Spell

A crescent moon hung low in the dark purple sky. A few stars still twinkled. Jack and Annie didn't move for a moment, breathing in the clean, fresh air.

Jack broke the silence. "It looks like we made it to Camelot before break of day."

"Yep. Where did we land exactly?" said Annie.

Jack turned on their flashlight. He pointed it out the window. The light shone on trees, their branches heavy with golden apples.

"I'll bet we're in the orchard where we landed

the last time we were here," said Jack.

"Turn off the light," whispered Annie. "I think I see something in the distance."

Jack switched off the flashlight.

A different kind of light was shining in the dark orchard—a flickering light that moved toward them. Jack heard leaves crunching, twigs cracking, feet running, and voices whispering.

"Jack? Annie?" a boy called out.

"Is that you?" a girl said.

"Yes!" cried Annie. She scrambled down the rope ladder.

Jack gathered up the jewel, the flower, the feather, and the panda bread. He put them in his pack and carefully climbed down after Annie.

Teddy and Kathleen stood in a circle of lantern light, dressed in their long dark cloaks. They hugged Jack and Annie. "Welcome!" said Teddy. "We have been walking the grounds all night, waiting for you. Finally we saw a light above the orchard!"

"Our flashlight," said Annie.

"And then we saw *your* light!" said Jack.

"We're so glad you're here!" said Kathleen.

"We are, too!" said Annie.

"Did you translate the last lines of the rhyme?" asked Jack.

"We did, indeed," said Kathleen.

"And did *you* bring the four things to help us break the spell?" asked Teddy.

"We did, indeed!" said Annie.

"They're all in my backpack," said Jack.

"Wonderful," said Kathleen. "We knew if anyone could find them, it would be you two."

"You have brought the four special things, and now we are all together. It is time to undo the spell," said Teddy.

"Yay!" said Annie.

"Yay, indeed," said Teddy. "Come along! Before the sun rises!"

Teddy and Kathleen started back the way they'd come, and Jack and Annie followed. Together, they wove between the trees in the fresh dawn air.

Finally they all emerged from the orchard. Kathleen shined the lantern on the door of a wooden cottage.

"Merlin's garden house," said Jack.

"Yes," said Teddy. "This is where we brought

Penny from her little nest in the castle. We hoped that she might come back to life in Merlin's favorite place. But alas, she has not done so." He sighed.

Teddy opened the door to the cottage, and they all stepped in. Jack shivered. It was damp and chilly inside, like a tomb.

Kathleen placed the lantern on a table in the middle of the room.

"There she is," Teddy said sadly.

Penny stood on the table, lit by lantern light. The little penguin was as gray and lifeless as stone.

"Penny?" said Jack. The last time he'd seen her, she'd been so cute, so warm and . . . alive.

"Poor Penny," said Annie. She touched the penguin's beak and the top of her head.

"Bring forth the four things you found to break the spell," said Teddy.

Jack reached into his backpack. "Here—this is the first thing we found. It's from India," he said. He took out the emerald cut in the shape of a rose. He placed the jewel in front of Penny, where it glowed in the lantern light.

"The emerald rose stands for love," Annie said. "The kind of love that rises above our faults and mistakes."

Jack pulled out the dried yellow and white flower and placed it next to the emerald rose. "This is from the Swiss Alps," he said.

"The glacial buttercup stands for being like a little kid," Annie said. "The joyful, open spirit of childhood."

"This is from Abraham Lincoln, a great president of our country," Jack said next. He took out the goose-feather quill and put it next to the flower.

"This quill pen stands for the deepest kind of hope," said Annie. "The hope that one day all our sorrows will make sense."

"And this is from China," said Jack. He took out the panda bread and put it next to the feather.

"This is called panda bread," said Annie. "It stands for protecting animals, for loving them and speaking up for them because they can't speak for themselves."

All four things were lit by the circle of glowing

lantern light, along with Penny.

"Teddy, stand closer, you're the spell caster," said Kathleen.

Teddy stood in front of the table. He closed his eyes and took a deep breath. Then he raised his arms and exclaimed, "All four things are here with me, the one who cast the spell. Spell be broken! Penny, come back to life!"

Teddy opened his eyes. Everyone stared at Penny, waiting for something to happen.

They waited and waited.

"Please, Penny . . . come back to life," whispered Teddy.

They all waited another long moment.

Slowly Teddy lowered his arms. "It's not working," he said quietly. "The spell to break the spell, it doesn't work." He picked up the small stone penguin and cradled her in his arms. "So you won't come back to us," he said. "You'll never come back to us." A tear fell from Teddy's eyes, then another.

"Oh, Teddy," said Annie.

Teddy wiped his face on the sleeve of his cloak.

"Don't look at stupid me weeping," he said.

"It's okay to cry," said Jack.

"Are you sad because you think Merlin will banish you from Camelot?" said Annie.

"No—no." Teddy shook his head. "I'm sad because . . . well, what you've shown us—what you said to us just now—makes me terribly sad. The emerald makes me think how much Merlin loves Penny, and your flower makes me remember the joy she brought to everyone. And your gray feather makes me think how desperately Kathleen and I have been hoping we could undo the spell and bring Penny back to life. And your panda bread makes me think how I was supposed to protect Penny while Merlin was gone. But I didn't care properly for her. I caused her harm instead. . . . I—I can't change that now. I can't, not ever, and I'm so sorry." As Teddy wept, his tears fell onto the stone penguin.

"Teddy," said Annie, "please don't . . ." But then she stopped.

Peep.

"Hush, Teddy," Kathleen said. "Stop crying. Listen."

Peep.

Teddy and the others looked at Penny. As they watched, the baby penguin's body turned from dull gray to soft white. She tilted her head. Her eyes blinked.

Peep.

CHAPTER TWELVE

One Penguin at a Time

"Penny! You came back! You are alive!" whispered Teddy.

"Hurray!" Annie shouted.

Teddy started crying again, but this time, he was laughing, too. Kathleen and Jack and Annie laughed with him, and the only tears now were tears of joy and relief.

The little penguin blinked and looked at each of them, one at a time. *Peep! Peep! Peep! Peep!* she greeted them, waddling up and down the length of the table.

Teddy picked up Penny. He rubbed his cheek against her fuzzy head. "It's a miracle," he said softly.

Trumpet blasts came from the distance. Startled, they all looked toward the window. Dawn light was creeping into Merlin's cottage.

"I'm afraid you must go now," Kathleen said

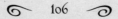

to Jack and Annie. "The sound of the trumpeters means that Merlin and Morgan have returned from Avalon. We could *never* explain all of this to them!" Kathleen laughed as she put the emerald, the flower, the feather, and the panda bread into a deep pocket of her cloak.

Then she looked at Teddy. He was hugging Penny and grinning as if in a daze. "Let us bring Penny with us, Teddy," she said. "We will lead Jack and Annie back to the tree house!"

The sun was rising when they left the cottage. Kathleen's cloak billowed behind her as she led them all through the orchard back to the tree house.

"Good-bye," said Teddy. "I—I thank you a million times. All of Camelot thanks you—or *would* thank you if they knew how you had helped me."

"Yes, yes, they would!" said Kathleen. She hugged Jack and Annie.

"Wait," said Jack, "what was the last part of the rhyme again, the part you just translated? Do you remember?"

"Yes, I do," said Teddy. Then he recited the words from memory:

When these four things come together
with the one who cast the spell,
the spell will then be broken
and all again be well.

"Oh, now I get it," said Annie. "*You* broke the spell, Teddy. You broke it all by yourself. By feeling all the feelings you felt for Penny, you broke the spell."

"Yes," said Kathleen. "I quite think that's what happened. The four things that Jack and Annie brought back did not break the spell. They only served to awaken feelings deep within you, Teddy. And that is what really broke the spell."

"Yes. You must be right," said Teddy. "I'm sorry you two had to go to such trouble to help me, and that Kathleen had to worry so. Not only Penny, but all of you suffered on my behalf."

"That's okay. We loved all our missions," said

Annie. "We helped an elephant find her baby. We helped a funny dog find out that he was a great dog, and a president find hope, and some pandas find their way home."

"All because you were trying to help Penny," said Kathleen.

"True," said Jack, stroking the little penguin. "It's weird how that works sometimes."

The trumpets sounded again.

"Hurry," said Kathleen. "They're getting closer."

Annie brushed her hand down Penny's back. "Bye, Penny," she said.

Peep.

"And *peep* to you," said Jack. He kissed the top of the penguin's fuzzy head.

Jack and Annie then scrambled up the rope ladder into the tree house. Annie grabbed the Pennsylvania book, while Jack hurried to the window.

Sunlight poured into the tree house, making it blindingly bright. Trumpet sounds filled the fresh morning air.

"I wish we could go home!" Annie said, pointing

to a picture of the Frog Creek woods.

"Farewell!" Teddy shouted from the dazzling light. "Thank you!"

The wind began to blow.

The tree house started to spin.

It spun faster and faster.

Then everything was still.

Absolutely still.

* * *

"We're back," said Jack. He and Annie looked out the tree house window. Dappled light danced in the woods. As always, no time at all had passed in Frog Creek while they were gone.

"Time for school," said Annie.

Jack groaned. He was exhausted. Every muscle in his body ached. He opened his backpack and took out their guide book to Southwest China. "Hey, we forgot. Our breakfast sandwiches are in here," he said.

"They must be cold by now," said Annie.

"Who cares?" said Jack. "I'm starving."

"Me too," said Annie.

Jack gave Annie a cold egg sandwich. Then he unwrapped his own and took a big bite. "Yum!" he said. "It really tastes great."

"This is *our* panda bread," said Annie, "made with love by Mom, one of our keepers."

Jack laughed. "Right."

"So the panda bread stands for protecting the pandas," Annie said between bites. "I think it stands for protecting birds, too, like Penny."

"Of course," said Jack, his mouth full.

"And trees and other plants," said Annie.

Jack nodded as he chewed.

"And dolphins and whales and fish," said Annie. "All the stuff in the ocean . . ."

Jack nodded again.

Annie finished her sandwich and wiped her mouth. "In fact, there are *millions* of things to protect," she said.

"Whoa, slow down," said Jack. He pulled on his backpack. "One panda at a time."

"Right," said Annie. "One penguin at a time."

"Right," said Jack.

The two of them climbed down the rope ladder. Then they hurried through the Frog Creek woods, finally on their way to school.

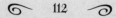

Author's Note

On May 12, 2008, the Great Sichuan Earthquake killed many thousands of people in Southwest China. Though the quake devastated the Wolong Giant Panda Reserve Center, all the workers and all but one of the giant pandas survived. The pandas have since been relocated to other panda reserves, until the Wolong Center is rebuilt.

News of the disaster in China brought a great deal of attention to the pandas, and support for these beloved animals increased.

Many organizations were already working hard to save pandas from extinction—groups such as Pandas International, the World Wildlife Fund, the Giant Panda Conservation Fund, and the China Conservation and Research Center for the Giant Panda. In fact, pandas have become a symbol for the protection of all endangered species of wildlife.

The panda's roly-poly body and innocent, shy eyes evoke feelings of awe and wonder, tenderness and compassion. Pandas seem to bring out the best in people. And that is only one of about a thousand good reasons why we should keep them living on this earth.

Mary Pope Osborne

WILL OSBORNE

Mary Pope Osborne

is the author of many novels, picture books, story collections, and nonfiction books. Her *New York Times* number one bestselling Magic Tree House series has been translated into numerous languages around the world. Highly recommended by parents and educators everywhere, the series introduces young readers to different cultures and times in history, as well as to the world's legacy of ancient myth and storytelling. She and her husband, writer Will Osborne (author of *Magic Tree House: The Musical*), live in northwestern Connecticut with their three dogs. Ms. Osborne is coauthor of the companion Magic Tree House® Fact Trackers with Will and with her sister, Natalie Pope Boyce.